PASSING

JUDGEMENT

Short Stories about Serving Justice

LESANN BERRY

ISINGLASS PRESS

Silverlake, Washington

ISINGLASS PRESS
PO BOX 1731
Castle Rock, WA 98611

Publisher's Note: This is a work of fiction. Names, characters, places, and incidents are a product of the author's imagination. Locales and public names are sometimes used for atmospheric purposes. Any resemblance to actual people, living or dead, or to businesses, companies, events, institutions, or locales is completely coincidental.

Cover Design by www.CreativIndie.com
Interior Design by www.BookDesignTemplates.com

Ordering Information:
Quantity sales. Special discounts are available on quantity purchases by corporations, associations, and others. For details, contact the "Special Sales Department" at the address above.

Passing Judgement/ Lesann Berry. -- 1st ed.
ISBN 978-1-939316-01-1

For Those Who Take Action

Concern should drive us into action.

–ANONYMOUS

Table of Contents

1 THE PRESIDENTIAL COLLECTION

SENATOR ALBERT COMMONS prepared to receive his guest by making certain the household was empty. Bothered by a flutter of unaccustomed nervousness, he permitted himself two minutes of pacing in the hallway, centering his thoughts on the achievement at hand. He'd sent his housekeeper out for the evening, presenting her with a pair of expensive play tickets in honor of her fifteen years of dedicated service.

Less than an hour later his caller arrived.

The subdued rap on one of the double front doors echoed in the foyer. Albert stumbled from his position on the bottom step of the sweeping staircase, stiff from waiting immobile. He approached the entry and, as always, experienced a surge of pride in the regal twin American shields carved into the massive panels. The coat-of-arms confirming his family's participation in the Revolutionary War was mirrored on the door exteriors so the public might be equally well-informed. He'd always believed the interspersed sprays of olive branches introduced an organic element that complemented the patriotic images.

He paused for a count of five seconds, one hand on the antique brass knob while he drew on the persona he'd honed over decades in public office. The man he prepared to admit to his home both frightened and fascinated him, but he'd been forced to deal with the reticent fellow. Solomon Lennard specialized in unique acquisitions. He accomplished what no other could achieve. The proof of his prior successes lay a short distance down the hall.

Albert greeted his guest and with a flourish, directed the visitor to proceed through the downstairs library doorway. Patience required effort but he wanted to draw out the moment and savor the anticipation even though he chafed to examine his prize. When his companion did speak, the man's speech patterns were precise and the enunciation flawless. Proof, Albert decided, of a nationality originating outside American shores.

He indicated Lennard should sit in the single Windsor chair and circled around to stand beside his ornately carved desk. Despite his resolve, the words burning inside Albert's mouth escaped, "You've been successful?"

Lennard patted the side of his overcoat with deft fingers. His lips curled in a satisfied smile. "I have it right here."

The compact object he withdrew was wrapped in startling white cloth. He laid the item on the leather desktop pad with a soft thud. With smooth motions he unfolded and pulled aside four layers of fine cotton. The last flap of fabric revealed an antique pocket pistol. The gun lay exposed on a monogrammed square of linen.

Albert salivated. "Remarkable."

Lennard nodded at the whispered word but said nothing.

Albert tore his gaze from the coveted sight to look fully at the procurer.

The man's stoic expression remained unchanged.

Dismissing the cool disinterest of his guest, the Senator's eyes stole back to the familiar form of the Philadelphia Deringer. A fierce jolt of satisfaction infused his body. He felt light-headed with triumph. His goal lay within his grasp, three of the four obtained. He stroked a finger along the short barrel, touched the grip with a reverential hesitance.

Albert dragged his attention to the man sitting a short distance away. "I am very impressed you achieved this task."

Lennard's eyes looked like dark holes in his long face. "I assume you find this endeavor worth such risk?"

"Assuredly." He bent to examine the small firearm beneath the yellow glow cast by the green glass shade of the desk lamp. He thought it a thing of beauty.

A percussion type handgun, the old piece had a caliber which ranged close to a .44 in modern terms, certainly capable of killing a man at minimal range. This particular gun had demonstrated that exact ability. The walnut grip, dimpled and cross-hatched with incised carvings, settled snugly against the palm. An intricate tracery of etched lines surrounded the stamped maker's mark on the flat top of the barrel. Rich German silver inlay banded a fierce eagle's head near the breech region and escutcheon. The front sight displayed a lovely dovetailed blade and fixed rear-sight tang. Even the lockplate and hammer were engraved with excellent foliate arabesque patterns.

Albert considered it an exquisite piece of workmanship despite the fact the detailed work was originally inexpensive, probably half of a set when purchased new. The gun reflected the artistry of a bygone era, an irony lost on most viewers.

Senator Albert Commons had memorized every facet of information concerning this pocket pistol. He knew everything there was to know about the events of that fateful night at Ford's Theatre and now he possessed the physical manifestation of a moment which changed the future of the country.

"I'm vastly pleased with your results; I should like to negotiate another commission." Without removing his greedy gaze, Albert touched the polished wood with a trembling digit, wondered if the fatal shot had been delivered by a sweaty finger or a hand held with cool concentration.

Lennard's voice came smooth as aged bourbon. "I am not indisposed to an offer."

The utter absence of inflection in the man's cadence unnerved Albert. The sound drew his complete attention. For a moment the shadows seemed heavier and denser around the still shape in the chair, the dark corners seethed as though an entity coalesced into a concrete shape. The Senator thrust away the fancy, cleared his windpipe and found to his disgust that his palms had gone slick with perspiration.

"I would like you to retrieve a final item of historical significance. The logistics are considerably challenging, more so even, than the recovery of the Lincoln derringer."

Lennard's gold signet ring winked in the dull light. "What singular object intrigues you?"

The mere thought of attaining the entire assemblage made Albert dizzy. The obsession to possess each of the firearms responsible for striking down an American president sent him forging ahead. "A Carcano rifle."

Lennard leaned back.

He was no more animated than the marble sculptures beside which the Senator had negotiated favors inside the gallery of the Rotunda.

After a silence lasting a full thirty seconds, Lennard nodded. "I understand. May I see the others?"

Pleasure ripped through Albert with a heat akin to sexual release but he cautiously considered the request, weighing the risk. His caller had demonstrated incredible acumen; why not indulge himself and share his achievements? After all, this man would acquire the crowning piece in his Presidential Collection.

Albert searched out and depressed a discreet button on the underside of his desk.

Both men turned to face the wall where a length of rosewood paneling cracked apart and slid open. Displayed inside was an elegantly arranged sequence of guns banded by a thick ebony frame. Two revolvers, a .32 caliber Iver-Johnson and a .44 caliber British Bulldog rested against a crimson velvet backdrop. Tiny titanium arms in the center of the case waited to cradle the Lincoln gun. Above was space for a rifle.

"The McKinley and the Garfield." Albert spiraled one veined hand to encompass the contents before he dragged his admiration from the exhibit to view the appreciation on Lennard's face. He jolted when he found the man still seated and the palm pistol pointing at his chest.

Lennard's lips twitched into an amused smile. "The Kennedy rifle always comes last. As you can imagine, the National Archives are a significant deterrent."

Albert swallowed hard.

The half-inch diameter of the muzzle directed at his torso took on the scale of a cannon mouth. He suppressed his momentary loss of composure and drew on pride to straighten his spine. Summoning the powerful voice that had given him an oratorical edge on the Senate floor, he voiced his fear in a demand. "What is your intent, Sir?"

The derringer barked. Smoke trickled out the breech. A burst of flame emitted from the barrel throat. The bullet tore a messy path through the fleshy skin in front of Albert's vocal organs.

"I'm the retrieval contingency." Lennard said.

◦◦◦

Solomon Lennard produced a padded sleeve from the interior of his coat and slipped each historic firearm carefully inside. The actions took only a minute to complete. He paused in the doorframe and surveyed the room. Nothing lay amiss, except for the Senator stretched out beside the desk and the pungent acrid odor of discharged gunpowder.

The door shut with a subdued click.

Two hours later he reigned in what little of his patience remained. He pulled on reserves as he faced the Senator's imperturbable legislative assistant inside the carefully appointed anteroom. The young man was difficult to rattle.

The aide adjusted the notepad at his elbow and offered another congenial smile. "I assure you, Senator Commons has never stayed at a lakeside motel in Wisconsin."

"Truly?" Solomon tossed one of the gloves on the conference table. The soft leather landed with a puff of air.

The aide's green eyes followed the movement but his curved lips never faltered. "Savile Row hand coverings are made of the finest doeskin." He smoothed a palm over one sleeve of his navy blue jacket and met Solomon's steady gaze. "I have a set of my own, a gift from the Senator to each of his top staff after he was reconfirmed into office last year."

Solomon appreciated the unexpected display of loyalty for Albert Commons, a man whose political antics ranged from the normal accusations of catering to special lobbying interests, to the more serious house sub-committee inquiry during the most recent election cycle.

"Your commitment to the Senator's reputation is commendable but unnecessary." Solomon leaned back in his chair and crossed his legs. He tugged the wool pant fabric taut above one knee as he considered his approach. "Albert Commons' presence in a tawdry motel in the company of a nubile young woman of questionable maturity is no longer of practical concern. I want access to the man's private office."

The aide leveled his fixed gaze across the desk. "I cannot accommodate your request, Sir, not without express approval from the man himself."

Solomon studied his companion and ignored the frustration curling in his abdomen. Unsurprised by the flat refusal, he felt a hint of curiosity about the lack of negative protestation or the demand for an explanation. A refreshing reaction, he decided.

The ticking of the pendulum in the elegant Seth Thomas grandfather clock echoed from the corner. The sole of a shoe scraped across the carpet. The aged wood frame of the antique chair creaked. Neither man capitulated their position.

Solomon opted for a more direct approach. "The Senator held in his possession an item which was not his own. I retrieve objects under the executive power of the highest level of government office." Solomon's right hand raised in a gesture to forestall speech. He allowed this information to be absorbed. After a pregnant moment he shifted his eyes to the clock and back to the aide. "Albert Commons is dead."

A brief display of panic crossed over the young man's features before the lines of his jaw hardened and his lips tightened into a flat line. Both changes in demeanor indicated the man had clenched his teeth.

Solomon continued speaking; his gaze pinned on the man. "In approximately seven minutes the Senator's housekeeper will return from a well-deserved evening out and discover his corpse on the library floor. Not long after, his staff will receive official notification."

The aide rallied. He schooled his features into another impenetrable mask of good breeding although his hands clamped tightly together, whitening across the knuckles.

Solomon scanned the space again. He contemplated if his surmise might be incorrect and decided his first conclusion, that the Senator had acquired another prize, was still the most logical. Three steps away from the garish front doors of the old house, the tableau had registered a discordant note. The Senator had presented his stolen firearms as though Lennard was an appreciated visitor, a guest to be impressed.

The performance had been successful.

The Presidential Collection had appeared dramatic. The spectacle of the quartet of guns, each responsible for killing a sitting Commander-in-Chief of the United States, was a macabre assemblage of political intrigue. The display board, lined with plush velvet and fitted with shiny brackets to hold the firearms, had been hidden behind an ornately carved cherry wood panel. The fifth set of prongs in the bottom middle had appeared to him as the space for an accessory or perhaps an inscribed plaque, a detail he hadn't connected until after he'd dispatched the Senator.

Sloppy work, in his opinion.

Lennard reasoned out the possibilities as he strode to the sedan waiting curbside. Plenty of assassination attempts had been carried out over the history of the country. The only other President shot during his tenure of office was Ronald Reagan. The .22 caliber pistol used by the gunman in that particular shooting had disappeared decades previously, a fact not known to the general public.

The Commons lineage had held political appointments for generations. They were a fixture in the Washington D.C. social scene, drawing on more than two centuries of interconnected relationships, favors, and influence. Solomon was confident he'd find the missing gun in the Senator's office space, an object so coveted it had ignited a desire to amass the complete collection.

The Senatorial waiting room was resplendent with framed art and fine furnishings. The hand-rubbed wood of the writing table between the two men glowed with polish. A faint odor of lemon and malt told Solomon the housekeeping staff employed British cleaning products. That figured. In Revolutionary times, the Commons' family had probably been Tory sympathizers. Even the intricate design of the Aubusson carpet cushioning the soles of his black wingtips featured the Senator's prized crest emblazoned in the pile. The room reeked with the subtle iconography of extreme wealth.

Aristocratic posturing at its American best.

The aide cleared phlegm from his throat and stiffened his shoulders. He rose to his feet, pulling an ornate fob from his pocket. "After reflecting on your news, I believe I may know where the Senator kept the item you seek." He crossed the room and fit the key into the lock on the interior door.

Solomon followed.

The Senator's personal office space featured the same sartorial elegance as the vestibule. Solomon swiftly located and opened the mahogany panels of the hidden compartment. The Reagan handgun lay nestled in a bed of green velvet.

"Everyone knew of the Senator's interest in young women –" The aide's voice trailed off as he watched Solomon slip the gun inside another of the padded cloth sacks.

Solomon Lennard tucked the bundle under his suit coat. "No one ever suspects an obsession with historic firearms."

The aide was young, perhaps twenty-five and his idealism was already tarnished. This town did that to people. He was probably the only son of an affluent family who'd spent a fortune to educate him at the finest law school and then bought an equally expensive appointment on Capitol Hill.

"What's your name?" Solomon canted his head and waited.

The aide's Adam's apple bobbed. "David Greene, Sir."

The Senator's untimely demise had shocked the aide but his resolve in the face of the unknown showed backbone.

Fingers wrapped around an object in his coat pocket, Solomon paused to indulge his curiosity further. "Where do you come from, Mr. Greene?"

A tiny frown creased the skin between the aide's eyebrows. "Lincoln, Nebraska."

Solomon removed the card and extended his arm, handing the rectangle of cardstock to the other man. "Call me if you're interested in employment. The job market is difficult right now and I could use a protégé."

The phone buzzed. Both men ignored the muted sound.

Solomon departed.

His last view of the room showed David Greene framed next to the grandfather clock. He was staring at the phone, the white card clutched in his hand.

2 LAST CHANCE FOR REDEMPTION

MITCH DRAGGED HIMSELF out of the swamp. His tattered camouflage pants streamed a trail of effluvia. Mud, blood, and mucky water trailed behind him in a filthy wake that marked his passage. He was glad to find higher ground. Slapping aside the reeds at the edge of the bank, he pulled his exhausted body up on dry land.

He cursed every ass-backwards Cajun who lived in this shitty bog, each of them intent on outlasting even hurricane Katrina.

The old woman hadn't died peaceably.

That always bothered him.

She put up a goddamned fuss though he was only doing his job. For Christ's sake, she'd shot his fucking leg because she wasn't ready to go.

Time's up, lady.

They never wanted to accept that fact.

When the time came, you went. Simple enough. Those were His rules. Mitch just did the enforcing.

A flash of bright color, a swirl of golden hair and the echo of a squeal of laughter filled his mind. His consciousness skittered away from the familiar thought and shut down that avenue of memory. He ramped up the anger, used the rage to keep from remembering, and refused to recall the details that carried him down this shit path.

He dug fingers into his palms until half circles of skin itched and burned beneath the pressure of his nails. The pain brought relief.

Think about *now* he ordered.

Mitch shook out his hands, watched mud and slime splatter against the hard packed dirt. After damn near six hours of slogging through bottomland, he'd found a road. He hiked up one canvas pant leg and inspected the three tiny pairs of puncture wounds on his calf. Almost delicate, the trio of red perforations marked the places where a determined cottonmouth had struck repeatedly. Each bite-mark was an objection to the disturbance Mitch caused as he struggled to hold the woman's head under the surface of the brackish water.

At seventy-three, the lady had been a real scrapper, a good fighter.

He appreciated a strong will but it was his job to persevere. Held down until murky fluid filled her lungs, her struggles had ceased. White hair, broken free of the tidy bun, splayed out from her head in a gauzy flow. She'd looked pretty anchored on a clump of cypress knees near the bank, in view of the porch. Maybe one of her worthless grandsons would come home early from a day spent poaching and discover her body before the gators did.

Mitch set out to receive his next appointment.

A ray of sunshine fingered down through the foliage but he dodged around the light.

No grace needed and no quarter given. He wanted none of that. They had a deal with fucking terms.

Buy salvation. Find solace.

Another flash of laughter and an echo of the word *daddy*...

Mitch broke and ran.

Hours later and miles down the road, he halted. His pants had dried. Blood from the gully left by the bullet had crusted over. He pushed up the long sleeves of his green army shirt, picked at the half-healed scab that never went away, flicked off a twist of dried grass, and studied the tattoo on his forearm.

The "d" in Danang was formed with elaborate curled edges and the lettered "sixty-eight" below the spread angel wings mocked him. So long ago now, but the lines looked as fresh as the night he'd drunk enough rice wine to let Patterson ink it on. At least infection didn't worry him anymore, not like then, when he'd been in the jungle and his arm had swelled up red and oozed pus for a month.

Eyelids drooping, Mitch stopped to rest. He propped his back against a weathered post, the long-forgotten marker for this abandoned crossroads, and waited.

That was the story of his existence now, an endless cycle of squalid murder and waiting.

A voice woke him.

Eyes gritty with sleep and dirt, Mitch blinked.

The figure of a man swam into focus. The sun hovered low on the horizon and a glow emanated into a haloed effect around the form.

Mitch snorted a derisive sound. "Hey, Boss. Save the theatrics for someone who gives a shit. We've already got a deal."

He ignored the patient sigh and heaved his feet up under his body to leverage himself into a standing position. Mitch stood at eye level, his demeanor adversarial regardless of how much he tried to restrain his anger.

The man's tone was soft. "All is forgiven, Mitchell."

Mitch tensed and shook his head. "Some mistakes can't be pardoned." He pushed the words out between clenched teeth. Shoulders stiffened, he narrowed his eyes in the glare of the sun and jutted his chin forward. "Give me the next task."

"Penance has a limit, my son."

Hands fisted into tight balls, Mitch shook with despair. "Not for me."

The silence stretched out. A minute passed.

Evening approached in the bayou and with it the buzz of insects and the drone of flies settled for the night. Mitch began to shiver, not from exposure or exhaustion, but from fear of the denial he sensed coming.

At last the man spoke. "It is time to rest."

Every word fell like a blow against Mitch's ruined heart. He *needed* these jobs, *wanted* the curses laid upon him, *de-*

sired the struggles of his victims as each experienced death. Shaken by the uncontrollable tremors vibrating through his body, Mitch's voice quavered with weakness when he uttered a hoarse denial.

"Just one more," he despised himself for pleading, "to guide, to show the way." The next one might absolve his guilt.

The sudden memory came too swift; he wasn't fast enough to close down the thoughts. The images bloomed. His little girl whirled in a circle, her hair spun out in a gilded ring, the pink and white frock floating around her like the inverted petals of a spring tulip...then the blood.

A guttural cry erupted from his throat. Mitch collapsed, palms over his ears, but still he heard her gasp when the bullet struck. His eyes clamped shut, failed to block the sight of her tiny body blown backward on the grass.

"The next might make the difference," Mitch sobbed, "be the one to balance the measure."

A touch gentled on his head, drew out the pain until Mitch breathed easier.

"You are not to blame, Mitchell."

The words brought a bitter laugh. "It was *my* gun."

After another long minute the hand fell away. "Very well. I will give you one final task, a last chance for redemption."

Mitchell raised bloodshot eyes; a tortured smile twisted his lips. "Tell me who to kill."

3 UNDER THE KNIFE

ISAIAH STUDIED HIS reflection in the mirror. This visit to Thailand had answered all his dreams. Now he wondered why he'd waited so long. Framing his face between his hands, he positioned his palms forward and stared at his features. For the last time he really looked, saw himself in this familiar and wrong way. His single fundamental flaw was soon to be corrected. In mere hours he would no longer be a woman trapped inside a man's body.

Relaxing his pose, he rotated slowly, his gaze following the shifting of muscles under his smooth skin. He didn't despise his male physique. He knew his anatomy appealed to others. He'd long ago accepted his attractiveness. In medical school he'd experimented enough to learn both men and women appreciated a healthy athletic form. Surgical reconstruction concerned more than his physical appearance, although having his outward looks reflect his inward reality would be such a gift. The decision to undergo reassignment countered other complex issues. This final step in his metamorphosis marked the termination of one life and the beginning of another.

He was about to be reborn.

This life-altering surgical procedure was a physical manifestation of Isaiah taking control of his future. Today represented the culmination of his journey as a male and the inception of his true self, the connecting of his spiritual entity with the sacred hoop of corporeal existence.

He slipped his arms through the loose holes of the cotton gown, tying together the frayed straps with ritual concentration. Even his escape from the sweltering stink of Miami for the wet heat of Bangkok seemed a symbolic rebirth. The sex-change operation was just the final stage in his transformation. Soon he would emerge from anesthesia-induced dreams, like a lunar moth bursting free of the cast-off chrysalis, reborn into a new life, a new identity, and a new world.

Just ahead lay the conclusion of a lifetime spent out-of-sync with every person of his acquaintance. The task of living as a partial human being rather than a whole had nearly ended.

Within minutes he was positioned on the table, a fresh-faced nurse chattering to him in the burbling consonants of the local dialect, smiling and patting his hand as she fit the pulse oximeter over his index finger. The pressure of the tiny device grounded him as the oxygen mask slipped over the lower half of his face. He inhaled deeply and sighed, a shiver of pleasurable anticipation rippling through his chest.

A movement caught his peripheral vision and he turned to find his physician smiling down at him. The laugh lines around her dark eyes crinkled into a fine roadmap, and at that moment, he thought her more beautiful than any other woman.

"This is the last stage of your journey, Isaiah." Her gloved hand smoothed across his jawline. His lips curved but his eyelids became heavy and his words of agreement were little more than a murmur.

The doctor's simple touch offered a comfort he gratefully accepted. His eyes closed. His hearing muffled. Isaiah's final thought before the darkness claimed him was that when he wakened, he would at last *be* Alicia.

◯⬯◯

Dr. Kanokwan eyed the monitors.

She watched the steady pulse signal for almost a minute and then concentrated on the EKG graph, counting the blips as they rose and fell in regular arcs. Every patient responded differently to anesthesia and she wanted the very best outcome for this special case.

Like all her American friends, Isaiah symbolized a connection to an important period in her life, relationships she had nurtured and cultivated over many years. One-by-one those old acquaintances and classmates had sought her out, once even a former professor had visited. She had particularly fond memories of her days with Dr. Teresseti and their long conversations about the challenges of plastic surgery.

Though each of them had trusted in her discretion, at the end of every visit she felt a bit lonely.

The sacrifices and deprivations her parents had endured to send her halfway around the world had proved worthwhile. Their struggle to finance her attendance at one of the finest medical schools in the United States produced unexpected financial windfalls after her return to Thailand. Ever mindful of her duty to provide for her mother and father as they grew older and yet more frail, she threw herself energetically into her medical practice.

The e-mail from Isaiah had lifted her spirits. Strict laws and intensive public scrutiny made medical procedures like this one virtually impossible in America. Fortunately there were no such restrictions in her country.

Part of her regular business model included communicating with former classmates and colleagues. She sent annual greeting cards, celebrating numerous holidays alien to her experience. She purchased expensive airfare to attend medical conventions every year and rubbed shoulders with learned peers to expand her circle of acquaintances. She never failed to issue warm invitations to visit her homeland.

Sooner or later, everyone wanted to explore Bangkok.

Dr. Kanokwan maintained a traditional peak-roofed house for just such guests. The kitchen was always stocked with American snacks and local fruit. The raised beds were fitted with hotel quality white linens. Every table was decorated with a bowl of fragrant flowers. The finest European wines poured into blown glass flutes by a house servant in the evenings. She made certain the villa hovered in a state of constant preparation and over the last decade she had entertained a steady stream of visitors.

In fact, Isaiah's arrival one week before was no longer the most recent.

Jillian Peters was settling in to the accommodations, having fled New York and her soured second marriage. She'd come seeking breast implants and a sampling of the sexual adventures on Nattapong Street. Unfortunately, there would only be time to experience one of those goals before her vacation ran out.

Dr. Kanokwan slanted dark eyes at the anesthesiologist.

"His numbers are good." The man said and adjusted down the mixture on the inhalation pump.

With a terse nod the doctor leaned down next to her patient's ear and squeezed his shoulder. "Goodbye, Isaiah." She whispered the words, kissed his temple, and smiled a tiny smile. Her educational experiences were about to pay unexpected dividends yet again.

She straightened and turned away, walked toward the exit, pausing at the door to speak over her shoulder in a clipped and clinical tone. "Harvest his organs and prep the room for the next one." She pulled off the nitrile gloves with a snap and dropped them in the trash receptacle. "These rich Americans make our work easy."

4 THE GIFT OF A LIFE

MESZAT CRUMPLED THE square of paper into a compact ball. The foolscap disappeared in the grasp of his large fist.

Squire Johnson's narrow face, instantly recognizable to him, had brought a surge of anger boiling up from his gut. The man's pinched pale eyes glared above the bristling facial whiskers on which the wealthy landowner prided his appearance. The illustration was like all the others Meszat had ripped down in the last twelve months.

Script he couldn't read covered the top of the wanted poster but he could guess easily enough what the words said. There'd been no need to include an illustration of *his* features. Like the other men of his village, he'd earned the marks of manhood when he came of age. Few who witnessed the scars pocking each of his cheeks forgot the distinctive rows of lines. The intricate patterns of raised tissue were memorable.

As soon as he'd arrived in this new land he'd learned his blue-black complexion and the wide tattooed bands circling his biceps were exotic and frightening, especially to white folk. He towered above most men and his appearance as well as his long strides drew attention wherever he walked. His face was well-known in the region around Squire Johnson's plantation. Even the resident populace along the waterfront of the nearby port towns recognized him on sight. The unusual cadence of his speech, a remnant of his African origin, identified his first-generation status and set him apart from most of the other slaves.

Escape had been long in coming.

Now he survived on his clever wits, living mostly in the wilderness. Occasionally he granted his fighting skills to the Maroon fugitives though their lack of organization boded ill for long-term freedom. Through the months, Meszat avoided recapture and carved out a life, but his desire for revenge never lessened.

Amidst a decade of slavery he'd made regular offerings of prayer and food, asking the ancestors for strength and endurance. He'd resisted temptation, outlasted torture, and survived sickness that engulfed others. Without complaint he performed muscle-tearing labor and tolerated the aches and pains of the harshest living conditions even as his spirit despaired.

In the end, the land itself tested his limits to the breaking point. At such times he worried the ancients had forsaken him. When the soil swelled with moisture and burst open, a crusted infection, suppurating like a diseased limb, he could no longer abide the dampness. The deprivations, cruelties, and hardships he faced without fear, but the climate weakened his resolve.

Eventually Meszat ran.

At first the Slave Code enforcers tracked him. They brandished chains and manacles, swarthy strong men with strange accents who spoke English no better than he. They followed him deep into the waters of bayou country. Laughter and coarse language interspersed their threats but Meszat had taught them caution.

He left the one-eyed leader draped over a column of Cyprus knees in the Okacheeta swamp. The second man had slashed with a wicked blade that served no good purpose when he landed between two alligators sunning on the muddy bank. The third pursuer he fed to the hungry river. After that, enthusiasm for collecting his runaway bounty waned.

No man mastered Meszat.

Travel took him into a northern landscape of rolling hills and then west into a world of unrecognizable trees, an unknown territory. He'd even caught sight of the wild Red Men outside their dome-shaped houses clustered at the confluence of three great waterways. The view speared his chest, a visual reminder of his own village that seemed like a memory of another life. He'd maintained distance, as wary of the inhabitants as they were of his presence.

Meszat found beauty in these new surroundings but the land lacked familiar scents and sounds. He craved the burning blue skies of home. He longed for the fierce wind to scour perspiration from his skin and sting his eyes with salt. He yearned to feel the blazing sun bake the soft mud of the ground into plates hard as rhinoceros hide but there was no way home to be found.

Freedom was not enough to fulfill his desires.

The frontier altered Meszat. His demeanor and carriage became that of the warrior destiny had decreed on the day of his birth. Time passed. The pressure built inside, urging him to return and face the thief who stole his life. One night his feet determined the right path and guided him back through the wilds.

He avoided detection and arrived in a familiar place, recognizing the waterfront slums of New Orleans. Several nights later he located Squire Johnson's townhome along the edge of the commercial district. Meszat recognized the squat shape of the multi-story house. He'd hoisted goods and portage from there to the offices of the Johnson Merchant Exchange Enterprises. The home was also conveniently close to the location where the man domiciled his quadroon mistress. It was the prime site to catch the man unawares.

A raucous sound of laughter jarred Meszat from reverie. He stepped back into the grime of the alley, slipping on the slick debris underfoot. A group of men, rowdy customers from a bawdy house exited an establishment to the east. He melted deeper into the passageway until the walls of the mercantile stores on either side pinched his shoulders. All around were warehouses. It was a familiar scene which offered him little comfort and held no warmth. The buildings sat filled with export goods awaiting transport to the docks and provided a secure place to hide away.

More nights passed before Meszat located his quarry, alone and vulnerable. He seized his chance.

Tall and strong, standing out among other slaves, Squire Johnson knew Meszat instantly. The night was early and the risk high, so Meszat slammed his fist in a fast blow and hefted the semi-conscious form over his shoulder.

The entrance of an adjacent building swung wide.

Meszat froze in mid-step. He'd struck down a Caucasian man, his *owner*. Panic prepared him for motion but a flow of energy reached out, surrounded and enveloped him. The warm essence touched him, became the familiar fingers of his blind mother searching his face for recognition. For a single moment he smelled the heat of Africa and heard his father's baritone laughter.

A dusky-skinned arm motioned him to enter.

Incapable of disobeying, Meszat bent low and carried his burden into the interior. The door latched behind him though a quick glance showed no person had done so. The inside was a dark cavern lit by a small clay oil lamp. His gaze dipped into the shadows where a woman stepped forward.

A length of bright fabric printed with tiny swirls of color wound around her body. Multiple strands of multicolored glass beads mantled her breasts. Both young and old, neither beautiful nor plain, she moved as if he dreamed. The high arches of her bare feet were exquisite.

She gestured at the floor and he obediently dropped Squire Johnson before her like an offering to a living shrine.

The man moaned and blinked. Blood gathered at the corners of his mouth and darkened his lips as though stained by blackberries but no words emerged.

Trying to meet the woman's eyes, Meszat discovered it impossible to focus, as though a delicate veil of spider webs obscured such intimacy. He perceived this female was more than human.

She pointed toward the street. "*Hamba.*"

Meszat stared, his shock complete. The woman spoke the language of his youth. She must be *Mchawi.* Fear filled him when she repeated the directive in a sharper tone and stabbed at the air with a long finger.

"*Hamba.*" She intoned a third time.

The hollow word spurred him into motion. He stretched behind and foraged for the knob, his hand grasping empty air. The skin at the back of his neck prickled. His heart pounded out a rhythmic pattern he recognized as the calling-forth-the-sky song the old men sang in his village.

The ancestors had answered his prayers after all.

The scenery shifted around the feminine outline in a hazy cloud, transparent like smoke. An echo of drumming hands filled his head. The sound was impossible to separate from the pounding heartbeats, the memories of his youth, and the dirt-floored room.

Meszat pulled air into his lungs and stumbled back a step. He believed this woman was more than a witch, an angry spirit perhaps, a vengeful entity come in response to his pleas. An echo of story bloomed in his memory, words told beneath the arching banyan branches while the midsummer moon hung suspended just above the horizon.

He knew her identity then and dread filled him inside.

She was *Haraka Shaya,* the one who strikes quickly, the bringer of justice, the eater of souls, and the demander of sacrifice.

"Meszat," the woman intoned, "I accept your tribute."

Mouth slack, he stumbled back from her terrible smile. Hand at last closing around the door lever – he pushed it wide and scrabbled backwards through the portal.

He shut his ears to the gurgling screams of the man who'd stolen years of his life. Meszat tried to pity Squire Johnson but found he could not.

The door slammed as if caught by a gust of wind.

All was silent on the cobblestoned street.

The evening air stroked his naked arms where Meszat stood with his hands limp at his sides. His soul felt bereft. The anger which had fueled his steps for the last year drained away, evaporating like river fog under moonlight. Retribution no longer mattered. Nothing of value remained in his mind. He longed only to hear *Haraka Shaya* speak his name, to see the words of his people spill from her mouth.

He dove into the gloom of an alley to seek the gift of a life.

5 Paying the Sin Forward

MALCOLM FITZ GLANCED over at his passenger as he pushed the gearshift into park and shut off the engine. The man slumped in the seat beside him looked like he'd worn the same grey suit for the last year. Every piece of clothing Brady Huffman owned was rumpled and creased in all the wrong places, which only proved Malcolm's theory that a cop was easily identified by his lack of fashionable wear.

"Your car is disgusting. You should just take cabs like us civilized folk do in New York." Malcolm said. He pulled the key out of the ignition and slapped dust off his pant leg.

Brady's responding grunt might have been an agreement but he said nothing more as he shuffled papers back into the case he hauled up from the floorboard.

"Tell me again what she does."

Brady bared his teeth in a tight grin. "She poses in the window of the building. She performs the same posture for an hour every Saturday morning." He jerked open the car door and exited.

Malcolm followed. He slammed the driver's side shut and hunched his shoulders as he lit a cigarette, shielding the flame with a cupped hand. His gaze darted around the neighborhood.

Definitely not an up-and-coming part of the city.

A trio of young men loitered at the nearest corner and two of the four closest buildings boasted faded *available-for-lease* signs that appeared at least a decade old. "The posing has something to do with her grandfather's bequest, right?"

Brady waited until Malcolm glanced over, then tilted his head toward the expanse of plate glass fronting the miniscule shop. A hand-painted sign above the bifurcated door read *Slipper's Folly.* "She maintains the weekly public appearance or forfeits her inheritance."

Malcolm waggled thick eyebrows at his former college roommate. "For a stack of cash, I'd perform a lot of stuff in front of the unwashed masses. Of course two decades ago I was such an exhibitionist I'd agree to pretty much anything for a six-pack."

Laughter rumbled up from Brady's chest, a sound like that of tank treads turning on ruptured asphalt.

The noise threw Malcolm back decades in time, to a dorm party and a tipsy redhead confessing how Brady's laugh made her want to whip off her blouse and fall into the nearest bed. Malcolm's attention snapped forward to his current surroundings when he caught sight of Meredith Slipper.

Brady noted his interest with a knowing smirk. "She's a looker."

"How'd you get drawn into this scene? You always disliked theatrics."

"Special orders from the top brass. My first case as a junior detective was running point for the head of the task force that investigated her grandfather's connections to organized crime. The old crew is all retired, so they pinned the job on me."

Malcolm cocked his head to one side.

"Things got interesting real fast." Brady said.

Exhaling a plume of smoke, Malcom's eyes traced up and down the female through the cracked glass panes of the dilapidated building. "How'd she take the news of her last remaining relative's demise?"

Brady pursed his mouth as he appeared to recall the conversation. "She sounded serene on the phone."

"So she wasn't close to the uncle either?" Malcolm sucked on the cigarette, his gaze glued to the shapely outline in the window.

"No."

Brady leaned back on the fender. They watched the statuesque woman remove her costume pieces. "He lived out in Phoenix since before she was born. Chicago's a long way from the desert." He straightened suddenly and shoved away from the car. "She's finished."

Malcolm dropped the Pall Mall butt to the stained pavement and crushed the smoldering ember underfoot. He crossed the sidewalk, pausing to stare at the tableau.

In the place where the woman had stood, a mannequin was now moved into position. He was struck by the eerie similarity in appearance between the live female and the resin form. A reddish-brown stole draped off one smooth shoulder, the mink luxurious and elegant, and a completely discordant note for the socio-economics of the neighborhood. Nevermind fur of any kind was scandalously unfashionable in today's world. A gilded masquerade mask flared outward from the temples into feathered wings. Champagne sequins caught light and reflected a scattering of golden droplets across a pristine white fencing helmet askew on a wooden shelf behind the figure. Lipstick colored the model's perfect rosebud mouth in the exact shade of red worn by the woman.

Malcolm shrugged off a shiver. "Who inherited the cash?"

"The old guy left his surviving son a cool ten million but nothing for the granddaughter."

Both men focused their attention on the sway of narrow hips as the subject of their discussion exited the exposed window display.

Malcolm grunted. "Too bad. A few mil would pay for some air conditioning."

Brady repositioned the handle of the briefcase dangling from his grip and stepped forward. "Arizona must have set new heat records because the uncle's bank statements show almost no money remaining in any account." He hesitated in the shallow portico and rapped on one of the age-rippled panels in the door. "Apparently the uncle liked to gamble."

"I thought this was a romantic story." Malcolm muttered.

Brady coughed to cover an inappropriate laugh. "No way. This is definitely a tragedy."

"I hate being the bearer of bad tidings."

"Liar." Brady tossed the word across his shoulder. "Reporters thrive on misery."

"I'll concede the point." Malcolm grinned. "So what happened?"

"Let me summarize. The short and sticky version is that her mother and father died in a plane crash. To everyone's shocked surprise the grandfather who had publicly denounced the couple and disowned his eldest son, turned an about-face and asserted his legal rights as next-of-kin. He stepped forward with wads of cash and a platoon of attorneys. He was appointed the custodial guardian. The girl had just celebrated her eighth birthday. The papers went wild. Philanthropic and humanitarian accolades were heaped on the old man. He established a household complete with an Irish nanny and private tutors, spared no expense on his granddaughter's education. To all appearances he denied her nothing." Brady half-turned to face Malcolm. "When the greedy buzzard died fifteen years later, there was a stipulation in his will that demanded she publicly humiliate herself as atonement for the sins of her parents."

"Sick bastard."

Brady nodded, face grim. "Makes you wonder how idyllic life really turned out to be for the poor little rich girl. The old bastard's plan backfired though. The granddaughter paid for a full-page ad in the society column and invited his business partners, their socialite wives, and the city's cultural elite to attend the grand opening of her ongoing performance. She proclaimed it the visual celebration of her parent's infamous love affair. It had steady attendance for the first year."

"Sounds crazy." Malcolm's voice carried a note of amusement.

Brady waved a finger in the direction of the surrounding offices. "Not as bizarre as the fact that in the thirty-six months since the grandfather's demise, she's collected absolutely zip besides the monthly rents on this crumbling structure. Lives no better than a pauper off the income. After five years of metropolitan penance, the deed reverts to her name. It's the only inheritance her obscenely wealthy grandfather left her."

"Guy sounds like a real jackass. He must have raised the girl with certain social and financial expectations, so why punish her for the actions of her father?"

Brady shrugged.

"What befell the rest of the estate?"

"Death and taxes consumed most of the assets but the liquidation of his landholdings net huge proceeds. Built his factories back in the twenties and thirties, acres of old processing houses squatted on the uptown side of the river are worth tens-of-millions now. Because he didn't designate a beneficiary, after probate is complete, the granddaughter will be declared his heir anyways."

Malcolm whistled his appreciation.

Brady adjusted the bag in his hand again. "Turns out the uncle, terror of rehab nurses and high stakes poker tables everywhere, also gifted his niece a tidy sum in a well-concealed investment account."

"Just how neat?"

"The whole ten million. We'd have missed it altogether if his attorney hadn't been puzzled by an unusual codicil in his living trust."

Malcolm was thoroughly invested in the story now, glad he'd flown out from Manhattan for this escapade with his old buddy. "Weirder than the criteria set out by the grandfather?"

Brady nodded. "In order to collect the balance, she has to make everything public." He tapped the satchel. "The details are here. The task must be completed by the end of the year. She meets the deadline or she gets nothing." As his hand stretched out to rap the door again, the brass sphere of the knob turned.

The portal swung open.

Malcolm swiveled to find the striking woman with auburn hair and deep brown eyes framed in the doorway. He took in the flawless complexion and ruby red lips before becoming mesmerized by the slight curve of her mouth. *A Mona Lisa smile.* His stomach muscles clenched at the thought.

"Detective Huffman?" The woman's husky voice intonated the formal address as a question. "I've been expecting you." She raised one finely arched brow at Malcolm with expectant inquiry.

Brady made the introductions.

Meredith Slipper appraised both men. "Please come inside. I assume you brought the documents found in my uncle's possession?" She took in Brady's sharp nod of agreement. "Your assistance is much appreciated. I realize Chicago PD's involvement up to this point has been a courtesy but as I suggested to the Chief, the presence of an officer of the law is just as important as that of my solicitor and a reporter." She laid a warm palm on the sleeve of Malcolm's shirt for a few seconds before indicating the satchel Brady had received from the Phoenix police department, "Inside that case is information I believe will identify the perpetrator of a terrible crime."

"Who's guilty of what?" Malcolm snapped out without hesitation. He sensed a story of scandalous proportions.

Fluttering long fingers for the men to follow in her wake, Meredith pivoted and began to move into the hallway. She glanced around once with her face in profile, a small cold smile curving her red lips. "I suspect there are detailed reports explaining how my illustrious grandfather committed murder."

Malcolm wondered if his old roommate had entertained identical suspicions all along. He jabbed his fist into Brady's kidney but the action only produced a mild grunt.

Brady motioned for him to follow. "Wait till you read the contents. You're going to be happy I called you for this exclusive."

6 BALANCING THE SCALE

THIS HAD BEEN one real fuck-all week for Detective Alonzo Rodriguez.

Monday started bad.

Tuesday ended worse.

He barely remembered Wednesday. Hump day involved stitches, bandages, and a dozen pleading phone calls to his soon-to-be-ex-wife. Thursday bled into Friday.

Now, plucking porcupine quills out of his left forearm, he wondered if this special torture anticipated more fun events for the coming weekend.

Every tiny fishhook barb pulled taut against his flesh, stretching the skin up in a pyramid before breaking loose. Each burned akin to a wasp sting. After the twelfth he almost welcomed the burst of sensation. The prick overrode the growling of his empty stomach and the persistent ache for fluid in the back of his throat. Every breath filled his mouth with red pulverized dust but he kept doing it anyway.

A groan punctuated his task and reminded him that he'd caught his quarry. Alonzo looked over, flicked a blood-tinged barb on the prone man's cheek and allowed himself a small victory smile.

David Chase would never run again.

Helicopter blades whumped a rhythm overhead and Alonzo aimed the last quill toward the dry streambed. The previous twenty-four hours had taken a physical toll but vital fluid had stopped seeping from the perimeter of his ragged field dressing. He figured the diagnosis was at a crossroads, being either a sign of healing or the mark of impending sepsis.

Goddamn he was tired. He craved sleep.

His prisoner gasped out a loose rattling moan.

Alonzo shifted in the rust colored dirt and eyed the fugitive. Spasms rocked the spree killer's body. The marks of sweat rivulets ran down his exposed skin but the man no longer perspired, was out of moisture to excrete. Coma would come soon enough and since Alonzo desired the bastard dead, he waited.

Natural causes were proving a bad way to die.

Deep in the backcountry, God had answered the detective's desperate plea and directed the wanted man across his path.

The helicopter roared past overhead, distracting his scattered thoughts. He closed his eyes against the swirl of dust. Tucked securely out of sight in the dense undergrowth, he estimated the machine would obliterate all signs of his passage. Bless the Feds and their toys.

Years of living in metropolitan Albuquerque had failed to erase Alonzo's ingrained childhood knowledge of the terrain or dulled his ability to read the climate. He sniffed the air. The complete lack of humidity in the canyon lands combined with high late summer temperatures to sweep dry wind between the scrubby trees. Exposure desiccated a corpse swiftly. Even animals would avoid the dried remnant of husk he planned to leave behind.

A pair of emergency flares sat shoved inside his shirt sleeve to signal the whirlybird once he was a distance down the arroyo. A necessity since he lacked the stamina to hike out. He was ready to go home but first he'd make sure the court system earned no second chance to screw things up.

His thoughts turned to Rachel. Brain too sluggish to reject the images, Monday's ugly scene played back similar to a jerky 8mm handheld film. She'd waited in the condo doorway, the credit card statement fisted in her hand. She'd circled the charges for the Cozy-8 Motel and the Chinatown Inn in thick black bands of ink. Her insults were screamed in English, Spanish and Croatian.

He'd deserved them.

Dressed in a form-fitting white sleeveless mini dress, she looked better than women half her age. He admired her tight ass when she sashayed down the stairs and exited his life.

Amused neighbors bore witness as his marriage collapsed, viewing the spectacle like a special episode of local reality television while he stood frozen in the doorway, fumbling to respond. He swallowed his denials, they were lies anyway. He drank much and slept little. Then bedlam exploded later that night.

Through a clerical malfunction of monumental proportions, the police department released a notorious killer from custody. The error thrilled the media. Reporters pounced on every uniformed officer for sound bites. News talkers gleefully reported how the cops let a murderer go free. The ass-kicking started with the top brass and traveled downstairs until nobody's butt escaped the departmental gangbang.

A thrashing gurgle caught his attention and brought Alonzo back to the present. He shifted his gaze to where the man convulsed, fingering the slash mark along his ribcage. He'd cornered Chase outside a convenience store on Wednesday but the cabrón had escaped into the desert in a stolen car.

Regret bit sharp.

Those teenage girls would never be the same. The three numbered among the reasons he held this vigil. David Chase suffered for them and all his other victims. Memory played the images in startling detail.

Alonzo shouted a warning but his words came too late. He'd watched the travesty occur as if time had slowed down. The trio of girls turned in synchronized motion like dancers in a choreographed show. Chase slashed each in his sprint to the driver's seat of the minivan. Pink Dress collapsed, tiny rows of scarlet flowers blossoming obscenely from her chest wounds. Blue Jeans blocked the knife with her arm, deflected the blow and lost two fingers for the effort. Yellow Shirt took a slice across her exposed midriff, an aborted C-section type scar that marred her perfect smooth flesh.

Chase gunned the engine as Alonzo caught the door, wrapped an arm around the side mirror and clung. Pain danced down his ribs as the vehicle lurched toward the road. The blade leaped again and thrust hard in Alonzo's shoulder. He fell amid the huddle of stunned targets. Weeping and terrified, the girls gathered around and staunched one another's wounds until the EMT's arrived. Blood puddled on the asphalt in a shining oil slick under the afternoon sun.

An APB located the van in the parking lot of the Ak-Chin Casino complex on the outskirts of the Sinagua reservation. Everyone groaned. Multijurisdictional squabbling allowed the quarry to slip through the law enforcement net again. Things complicated fast. The pursuit became a federal game when the major crimes division brought in the FBI.

The general public didn't know the details about Chase's desperate need for insulin. Detective Rodriguez knew. He was also capable of tracking the bastard deep into the desolate back country.

The thrashing slowed and then stopped. The shallow movement of the man's chest, rising and falling in the evening light stilled. No dramatic denouement occurred. David Chase died quietly. Painfully.

Alonzo discarded the corpse under the salt cedars. He climbed to his feet, swayed in the deepening gloom and stretched stiff limbs. Head cocked, he listened to the chopper shift direction for the return sweep. He walked carefully between the rocks, staggering a bit when the slope began to climb, and followed the barely discernible game trail. A half mile he estimated, to the mesa top where the bird could land. He might make it after all.

He stumbled, swore and recovered his balance. For a moment he thought about his wife and missed her. Mostly he just felt thirsty.

7 THE TSAR'S GRANDDAUGHTER

IVANKA DAVIDOVITCH BOUGHT a lottery ticket at one minute after ten in the morning. The Megabucks Shooter's Jackpot offered two chances to win, a string of numbers on the "A" line and a second list on the "B" line. The odds were lousy, less than three-in-a-million, but as she pointed out to old Mr. Titov behind the counter, somebody had to win.

"Why not you, eh?" The old man asked, punctuating his smile with a clack of his false teeth.

Why not indeed?

She might be the sucker born twenty-two years ago, but today was her birthday, her lucky day. Her father had said so with a kiss on her cheek before he sent her out the door.

She walked out of the corner market with half a green burrito clutched in her left hand and the lottery ticket in her right. She was looking at the two lines of numbers for no real reason when she bumped into a man wearing a hat.

The stranger had just stepped away from the payphone, the one everyone used to call tips into the cops, dial up their drug dealer, and pretend to be concerned citizens when a fire lit up the night. The neighborhood kept to itself. She knew the guy in the hat didn't belong. He stared at her with a funny expression and reached for her arm. She pegged him as a debt collector, probably hunting her old man. No matter how many times he said he'd done with the gambling, the cards and dice lured him back. Ducking sideways, Ivanka avoided the grasping hand and slipped around the bumper of Jimmy Nikolav's cab. She crossed the street.

Hat Man followed.

Ivanka turned to the right and shot inside the Russian deli, shouting good morning to the proprietor as she dove for the rear exit. Mama Stepanovna had changed her diapers as an infant, wiped her nose during the tomboy years, and swatted her teenaged head when she'd talked rude to an adult. The woman would recognize the possibility of pursuit and fill the empty wake of Ivanka's passage with her considerable bulk. The stranger in the hat wasn't getting past the matriarch whose grandmother had once attacked a Bolshevik party official with a pitchfork.

She evaded the collection unit and reached the apartment to discover the door busted wide. The interior was empty, her father gone. The quantity of blood smeared across the floor raised her worst fears.

Ivanka swallowed hard. She skirted the puddle of garish red liquid and spent twenty seconds of valuable time grabbing her escape pack. The stairs to the roof pounded hollow beneath her feet. She dialed a number on her throw-away cell phone, the cheap plastic numbers creaking under the pressure of her index finger. The ring sounded twice before someone answered. They offered no greeting, only listened.

"Collectors came for Davidovitch." She gasped out the words and shoved hard against the warped fire door.

"Meet me at the corner."

She mashed the disconnect button and ran to the far side of the rooftop. She located the plank bridge that spanned the gap to the neighboring building. The office complex, a remnant of an unsuccessful urban re-edification attempt offered the adjacent roof level as a community garden. She lunged across the wide boards, ignoring the six-story drop to the narrow filthy alley below. She squeezed between the rows of tomato bushes and aimed for the stairwell access.

A car would be waiting at the street level in a matter of minutes; she just had to reach that relative safety. She tightened the straps on her backpack and thought for a fraction of a second about the man who'd fathered her. He'd been an absentee parent for the last few years but it hadn't always been that way. To her surprise, a tear spilled down her cheek.

She was an orphan now. Well, as much as any daughter of the Russian District was allowed to be, since the community was family too.

Her grandfather would determine the source of this threat. Always manipulating the municipal political system, trading favors with the Italian and the French organizations,

cementing the boundaries of his three-block empire, he wielded power.

The man in the hat might have been Italian. His coloring
had been dark but he could just as easily be Georgian or
even Croatian. Waves of eastern bloc immigrants had flooded
to America in the last decade. Everybody vied for more trac-
tion in the city.

She wanted to call Johnny. They'd planned a private
dinner tonight to celebrate her birthday. Right now she
needed to hear his voice but first she required a route down
to the street level.

Her boots rang against the asbestos asphalt tiles covering
the steps. The stairwell canted back and forth, a small land-
ing at each half-level. The rhythm of the cadence caused by
her descent formed a complex syncopated pattern that filled
the concrete column like a primitive hand drum in an echo
chamber.

She glanced at her wristwatch. Seven minutes had
elapsed since she abandoned home.

Her father must have known.

The realization made her steps falter. Davidovitch had
deliberately sent her out to get the lottery ticket even though
he knew she planned a trip to the market after lunch. He'd
wanted her out of the house. Another tear leaked out and
trickled down her face. She swiped it away.

Two more floors.

Four sharp turns.

A shout echoed high overhead and stopped her dead.
Had someone followed her across the roof? She scurried
through the second level exit into an empty hallway. The
door shut on the stairwell but she heard the bellows of angry

men as the gap closed. The sounds drifted up from the ground floor.

They had her trapped inside the building.

She darted down the hall and crashed against the propped-open door of Petrov's Insurance.

Irma Petrov flinched but her eyes never lifted from the document on her desk. The woman's fingers continued tapping on the keyboard, the angle of her face turned away from the entrance.

Ivanka grinned as she slipped past the secretary. What Irma didn't see, she couldn't be forced to admit.

The fire escape offered the best chance now. She slithered through the narrow crank-out window, her backpack scraping against the metal frame. The street looked farther away than she'd thought. No time to waver. The steel fretwork clattered under her feet, the rusty platforms creaking as she descended. The palms of her hands felt gritty. Bits of paint flaked off, along with the grime that accumulated in the inner-city.

Something big was happening. This sort of interest involved a prize greater than her dad's gambling debts.

⊙❦☙

Exactly how much money made a person sinfully rich?

Ivanka wanted to pose the question to the model-thin waif of a female attached to her grandfather's arm. The woman appeared three, maybe four years her senior and was no doubt prowling for a keeper. In the ten minutes since her arrival at the house, her grandfather had not spoken once or looked at her.

LESANN BERRY

By contrast, the ornament on his arm chattered incessantly. Her rounded vowels indicated a Polish or Serbian ancestry Ivanka didn't care about, except she wanted to recall the words for shut up.

The backpack containing her critical possessions trailed from one hand as she followed the mismatched couple into the dining room. The Tramp prattled on about some other famous performer, also sinfully rich, who tugged at her materialistic heart.

Ivanka mimicked the woman's pronunciation in her mind, dodging the finger of awareness trying to pin down the questions tumbling around in her brain. Her knees hadn't stopped wobbling from the climb down the fire escape and the frantic dash to the familiar black sedan waiting at the corner. The embassy emblem of the Russian state seal on the side of the sleek Mercedes, a common enough sight in the neighborhood, drew little comment from passersby.

Although everyone noticed.

She almost felt the collective sigh of relief go up when she slipped through the open rear door of the vehicle and saw Borgrav behind the wheel.

His steel grey eyes searched for hers in the rearview mirror and nodded as she slammed the lock shut. His shoulders filled the front compartment. The muscled bulk of his presence was familiar and comforting. He served as the family heavy hitter, literally. Before being pressed into diplomatic service by her grandfather, he'd been a professional boxer for the Red Army, renowned for breaking men's jaws with a single blow. Officially he was her godfather, charged with the responsibility of seeing she was raised with a proper respect for God. He was also her uncle.

As an atheist he'd failed in the first regard but never in the second.

He'd driven to the house and handed her from the car at the rear entrance, patting the top of her head just as he had when she'd been a little girl. He sent her inside with a bit of advice. "Be patient with him, Ivanka. He tries to understand this modern desire for independence but he does no better now than he did with your mother."

Without Borgrav to mediate tempers, she and her only grandparent would have fought and disagreed even more, if that was possible.

She realized her grandfather had dismissed his mistress and acknowledged her presence. She nodded agreement to his offer of Vodka and collapsed on one of the high-backed chairs at the formal dining table. For as long as she could remember, important business had always been conducted in this room. The expanse of polished wood sat twelve and as soon as guests settled into their seats, food would begin to appear, trays and dishes of Russian delicacies shuttled in by one of the silent servants. The staff was imported from the homeland and none spoke English. Were it not for that strict rule, her own mastery of the mother tongue would be lacking.

"Why do strange men pursue me through your district, grandfather?" In her distress, the syntax of her sentence became jumbled but he did not correct her.

She accepted the glass of clear liquid he offered and slumped into her seat, resting booted feet atop her backpack.

Her grandfather's face took on a pained expression.

"You grow more like your mother. Always she worried first about Davidovitch, then herself." He sat at the head of the table and studied her intently.

Ivanka smiled at the familiar complaint. Here was a diplomat with no diplomacy for familial relationships. Borgrav had once confessed that her long-dead grandmother had berated her husband for preferring conspiracy and intrigue to honest work.

Personally she thought he excelled in both.

"You are safe here. Men search the streets for strangers. There is no word about your father, I am sorry."

The last three words were somewhat stiff but the fact her grandfather had spoken them at all told her everything she feared was likely to be true. Ilya Davidovitch had never been good enough for the daughter of an ambassador, a man with important political affiliations. Ivanka's mother had married him anyway. The marriage had been happy, if brief. The cancer diagnosis shocked them all; the disease ravaged her body, unexpected, vicious, and incurable. Even the American Tsar failed to defeat such a foe. He raged at the doctors, helpless as the wasting illness that took his wife also stole his child. Ivanka was the gift that came from tragedy, the uneasy truce between the men who loved her and shared a monumental loss.

Her father had never recovered either.

"Davidovitch knew someone was coming. He sent me away. Why?"

Her grandfather's gaze fell and she realized with sudden insight that he was hesitant to explain.

Ivanka went to his chair and knelt on the floor at his feet. "Tell me the truth, grandfather."

He sighed. "It is not good, my granddaughter. Your father agreed to steep terms even though he could not meet them. The outcome of dealing with these unpredictable Croatians has finally cost him dear. That is the price of his gambling."

The confirmation stole her breath. "They killed him?"

"Perhaps."

Her lips felt numb but she sensed there was more. "What do they want with me?"

After another uncharacteristic hesitation he explained.

The words echoed in Ivanka's ears. She knew the phrases. He reeled off explanations of negotiated marriage contracts, the importance of meeting obligations to the family, the community, the future. In old Russia, daughters had always been commodities, traded and exchanged for favor and influence, used to cement alliances and defuse violent disputes.

She reeled back from his stern face. "You are a stranger to me." The whispered words did nothing to dispel the horror in her tone. "You cannot be serious."

He was.

Her grasp of the language failed and she cursed in English. She scrabbled away from the table, heels dug into the deep pile of the Turkish rug. Her back bumped against the drink cart and a decanter tumbled over, crashing onto the silver tray with a clatter. Ivanka pushed off the wall with one palm, scooped up the strap of her pack and was on her feet and stumbling out the door before her grandfather rose from his chair.

He called after her in a voice hoarse with emotion.

She fled through the interior. The Tramp stood at the base of the grand staircase, a speculative expression on her face as Ivanka shoved open the ornate leaded glass front doors. Muffled shouts followed her but she barreled down the walk and burst between the iron gates. Half a block away one of the busiest boulevards in the city offered the congestion of traffic and the concealment of pedestrian crowds. She pounded past the uniformed security officers in the barricaded kiosk and reached the corner, disappearing from view almost instantly. She didn't stop running until she was exhausted and lost. The signs on the tiny storefronts advertising variations on traditional staple of kimchee told her she was deep in the heart of the Korean District, a place controlled by men who did not deal with her grandfather. Instinctual flight had bought her a brief moment of safety.

The phone in her pocket buzzed. She leaned against the dirty brick wall of a company advertising imported goods and checked the screen. *Borgrav.* She hesitated. This morning she would never have questioned her uncle's loyalty but after her grandfather's betrayal, she might as well face the worst possibility.

She answered. "Did you know?"

The silence said he had.

When he spoke his voice was grave. "You must remember that the older generations never chose their spouses. Even the great Kolya Todorov married a woman selected by his parents."

She hadn't known that fact about her grandfather but it didn't matter. "This is not the old country, Borgrav. I refuse to satisfy his misplaced sense of tradition and marry into the community that may have killed my father." Her voice broke and the street suddenly seemed empty.

Ivanka slipped down the alley next to the brick building and emerged onto an even narrower lane. No one paid any attention to her presence but she understood they were as aware of her as she had been of the stranger in her own neighborhood that morning.

"Come back to the house, Ivanka. Make peace with your grandfather."

"He never forced my mother into an arranged marriage – " She cut down another alley, realization dawning. "He's not giving me a choice, is he?"

The silence grew on the line.

"He can't force me to do anything." She said.

"Sadly, that is true." Borgrav agreed. He grunted in her ear. "You're right, Ivanka. We do not live in the old country but some things do not change. He believes this is for your best interests, a way to consolidate family strength and look to the future. You should know he tried to negotiate on Davidovitch's behalf. His efforts were rejected."

A chill settled in the pit of her stomach. She lived in the insulated comfort of her neighborhood, under the benevolent umbrella of her powerful grandfather. She didn't pay much attention to the news but like everyone else, she'd heard about the Croatians venturing below Sixtieth Street. They canvassed the bars and roughed up the local toughs. The posturing was an attempt to evaluate the vulnerability of the smallest of the ethnic enclaves in the city. They were not really threatened by the possibility of a takeover. She was almost sure.

Ivanka stopped in mid-stride.

Color stained her cheeks. She needn't think the worst of her grandfather. To him this alliance would make the best sense, a way to see her settled, create a valuable link between the two districts and maintain his own domain as a separate political and cultural entity.

"This is not frigging 1930!"

The familiar rumbling laugh reminded her Borgrav was still listening at the other end of the phone connection.

"Give the idea time to register, Ivanka. Combining houses is not such a poor thought. Have a coffee. Consider the future and call me back. I will come get you."

He disconnected.

She'd been busy *combining houses* for months. So much for trying to be discreet.

Borgrav had done his best to soothe her fears. Ivanka thought she understood why. She pulled up a mental map of this corner of the city and measured off the different districts. To the north were the Croatians. The Italians held the south. The French ruled to the east. On the west side, in her present location, was the Korean community. Theoretically speaking, she had already picked a groom among the sons of Italy. The Cosa Nostra was well-established and operated on a similar sense of honor that resonated with Russian etiquette.

She had been introduced to the patriarch of the American branch of the Sicilian family six months ago. Borgrav had presented her to the *cosca* leader during their attendance at a wedding celebration. Addamo Salvati was even older than her grandfather but he smiled with genuine amusement while Borgrav rattled off her entire formal name as if they were at some state event. She'd been embarrassed when the old gentleman referred to her as the Tsar's granddaughter and showered compliments on her beauty and the importance of familial connections. She'd escaped as soon as Giovanni Fiore asked her to dance.

They had attended the same private high school but since neither carried the surname of their infamous grandparent, they hadn't placed the association. Once they figured out the connection they became frequent party partners after the event, meeting often in nightclubs and hotspots around town. Now she whipped her phone from her pocket and scrolled through the listing until she found Johnny's number.

He answered on the second ring.

An hour later she was relating the details in person to Mr. Salvati while sitting at his fourteen foot dining table. Giovanni sprawled in the chair beside her and clasped her hand under the tablecloth as she relived entering the bloody apartment and her subsequent escape from the office complex. When she finished speaking, the old man wrapped his hands around a white porcelain mug, so hot that steam rose from the contents, and sat silent for a long moment. His black eyes moved from his grandson to her and back again.

Directing a fond smile at her, the elderly man turned and spoke rapid Italian to Giovanni. After the flood of speech ended he motioned for them to leave. He was reaching for the heavy old-fashioned phone receiver as Ivanka was escorted from the room.

As soon as the door closed behind them Ivanka was pulled into a fierce embrace. Too stunned to respond at first, she stood with her lover's arms wrapped tightly around her torso, then she began to quiver. Tears slid down her cheeks. She did nothing to stop the grief. The weeping didn't last long. She'd loved her father but had no illusions about his faults. There would be time to mourn later.

"Thanks Johnny."

He must have felt her relax because he shoved something hard into her palm as he whispered in her ear. It was her phone. "Go into the study and call Borgrav. Tell him not to hit me after I ask your grandfather for permission to marry you."

He left her there in the hall.

Tear tracks still wet on her face, a smile turned up the corners of her mouth. Ivanka watched him stride out the front door, the .38 snub-nose revolver tucked into the back of his waistband as insurance. She was certain her grandfather would be pleased by the potential value of an alliance between their families.

Her father had been right. This was her lucky day.

It wasn't until after the phone call was complete that realization struck. She wondered just how long the two old men had conspired to design this drama.

8   Passing the Kill

DUARTE CAVALERA FINGERED the plane ticket in his pocket. He'd carefully stowed the heavy cardstock in the interior compartment of his black suit coat and the stiff paper made a shussing sound as he half withdrew and then reinserted the boarding pass. He was ready to depart. He missed the humidity and the food. He desired to hear the cloying voices of his native tongue, the endless fractured clattering of the millions who also called Mexico City home.

Mostly he did not want to kill this girl he watched. Did not want to see this pretty child, on the very edge of becoming a woman, stumble and fall with her arms outstretched as a bullet crashed through her cranium and furrowed inside her brain.

Too young.

No more than months separated her in age from his youngest child. With her dark hair and eyes, she even resembled his Tania. Her friendly smile flashed readily, offered equally to the skateboarders veering down the walkway and the homeless man who responded with a crass comment.

He'd address that too before he left for the Houston airport.

Yes, he was a veteran in this industry and had a reputation to protect but this would not be the first time he'd refused to complete a task. Past consequences proved stiff. Twice before he'd re-evaluated options once he'd studied the target. He'd learned to trust his instincts. Many opportunities arose to kill someone but after the job was finished there was no way to reconsider.

Pushing aside the ticket with his forefinger, he grasped his phone and pulled out the device. He touched in the six digit code to open a browser, pleased by the wonders of modern technology. With a device like this no one needed .007 anymore.

So much change in the years since he began his career path. Word had gotten around but the real hard cases, the clients who believed money bought any deviant act, they never learned. Some simply refused to accept limitations even existed in this brave new world. Every man had a line he would not cross. The code of ethics might feature shifting boundaries but lying to a professional killer was inadvisable and he suspected his client had done so.

The log-in sequence opened an encrypted website. He slid spectacles into position and peered at the tiny screen. He accessed contact information and typed in a few key words. Data streamed past in a column and he looked away. Time to have his vision checked again. Close-up focusing against the black background fatigued his eyes. He turned for another surveillance of the girl and made his decision. He was passing the kill.

She walked in the company of other students, the grey concrete edifice of the college library framing the scene. The small figures disappeared into the building and the clock tower began to sound the chimes announcing the half hour.

He reviewed his phone, studied the name and address on the screen and nodded. Mexico must wait. He needed to visit Southern California first.

⊙≋

A thousand miles west and a day later, Duarte sat across from the client who had hired him to shoot Angela Dixon. The physical similarity between mother and daughter was readily apparent and ended there. He'd spent an hour with Angela and her friends in the campus library last evening and he'd come to know the young woman's open friendly face. She evidenced an honest and helpful personality. Her eyes were filled with light and energy, a desire to help the world, and she had a plan.

That was the crux of the issue it seemed.

Angela's father had died several months before and once the lawyers finished sorting out the details, she stood to inherit the bulk of his substantial estate. The mother, divorced and in financial straits, wanted a taste. She disapproved Angela's plan to establish a philanthropic organization to oversee the distribution of funds to various worthy causes. Duarte figured mommy hungered for the whole pie. In legal terms she would be declared her daughter's sole beneficiary.

He decided a personal visit offered the strongest deterrent to further forays down the assassination path.

"I only have a moment before I meet with my next client, Mr. Duarte." She flashed an insincere smile across the desk.

He crossed his legs and rested his clasped hands on his knee. "It is just Duarte."

She nodded, clearly not interested in his name.

"What can I do for you?" She asked.

He let the silence stretch out until he knew the woman had begun to wonder about his presence. "You hired me to put a bullet through your daughter's skull. I am canceling our arrangement."

She went rigid in her chair. Her hands curled into claws on the desktop and a denial half-formed on her lips.

He continued. "The fee I was paid will be the inaugural donation received by the philanthropic organization Angela plans to establish when her inheritance comes to fruition. I believe a parent should always take pride in their child's efforts to make the world a better place. This is your way of making a final contribution."

He paused for a response but the woman's face remained stony.

"In future, you must not seek to injure or bring harm, or serve as an instrument of danger to the health or wellbeing of Angela Louise Dixon. Should severe illness, accidental injury, or inexplicable misfortune befall Miss Dixon, I will assume those acts to be of your doing and take appropriate retaliatory measures."

The former Mrs. Dixon might be a real-estate guru and accustomed to hiding her emotions from histrionic clients but she failed in this regard. To Duarte, her pale features were a mask of anger and fear. *Good.* He believed he'd made his point, so he rose to his feet.

Her gaze followed him, eyes wide. The pulse at the base of her throat fluttered faster when he adjusted his suit jacket and she glimpsed the handgun in the underarm holster.

"I don't know what you're talking about, Mr. Duarte." The words issued in an emotionless stream.

If her lips hadn't parted he wouldn't have been certain the denial emanated from her mouth. "I do not require an admission of guilt, madam, only your acquiescence." He halted with one hand on the polished nickel hardware and gave her a hard stare. "I will be taking a personal interest in Angela's good works for many years to come. How unfortunate that the growing demands of your profession make time spent together an impossibility."

Duarte exited and closed the door gently behind him.

He would remain in town and monitor the situation, determine which route was optioned. He hoped the mother chose well. He did not savor making any child an orphan, but sometimes loss built character. Angela was already a remarkable young woman; another tragedy in her young life might pave the way for even greater gifts. Either way she would survive and thrive.

9 THE REVEREND MR. BLACK

L AINIE SEARCHED FOR the vintage record, flipping through the stacks of dusty cardboard sleeves while she waited for the Sheriff to answer the phone. The Bitterwater Sheriff's Office had once served a thriving town but that was back before the granary shut down. She'd read about the exodus of people leaving rural farm communities for the big cities. In recent years the population of her tiny Nebraska hometown hovered steadily at 1,495 hardy souls. She adjusted the number each time it became necessary, after studying the obituaries posted on the county website every Sunday morning.

On the seventh ring someone picked up with a clatter. A gruff voice wheezed into the receiver, barked out an official title.

"Sheriff Dunsteady?"

"You got him."

She went straight to the facts. "Celeste Dupre was my mother; she disappeared from Bitterwater ten years ago. Her husband, the Reverend Mr. Black has just confessed to her murder."

An inarticulate splutter of air told her she had the Sheriff's full attention.

"Where are you calling from?"

Pinning the antique receiver against one shoulder she plucked the tattered album from the pile and grinned. "I've come home, Sheriff. I'm here in the house."

The sound of papers shuffled. The clunk of something being shoved across a desk carried through the phone. She sensed his intense alertness, imagined him tuned into their conversation like a bird dog on point.

"Is your stepfather there with you? Can I speak to him?"

Lainie's gaze shifted to the open doorway of the kitchen, to the dark trouser cuffs neatly folded above the polished wingtip Oxford footwear. The visual evoked a sense of nostalgia. She liked the shoes. The uneven tapping of fingers fumbling on a keyboard drew her attention back to the call. "I'm afraid the Reverend is beyond the reach of earthly words. You see, he's found salvation in the work of the Lord."

The silence was so abrupt it echoed. "Tell me what you done, Lainie Dupre."

Pulling the shiny black disk from the musty cardboard, she slipped the circle of plastic over the bright silver nub of the turntable and set the needle gently on the groove. A scratchy muffle preceded the twang of banjo strings and then the mellow voice with its warm soothing tone washed over her and a wave of sentimentality swallowed her senses. For a fractured moment she was carried back in time, the music transporting her over the years.

"You know that idea from the good book, the one about an eye-for-an-eye?" She received an affirmative grunt and continued. "There you go, Sheriff. I've been courting biblical vengeance." After that the Sheriff got real quiet and listened until she stopped speaking.

He asked her some questions and she answered truthfully but had trouble concentrating. The song pulled at her, brought to mind powerful images of her mama humming along to the words. The record had played over and over back in those days. The reminiscing filled up her insides and drowned out the hollow echoes.

Mama had prayed her husband would become that gentle man in black. He hadn't.

"Deputy Williams is turning off the county road. He's almost there, Lainie, do you hear me?" The Sheriff barely paused for a response. "He's going to get you out of this situation. Don't resist or make a fuss."

She ignored the urgency in his voice and sang along with the chorus, smiling, weaving her hips to the music, side-stepping the bloody rivulets seeping across the hardwood floor. The reverend in the song was patient and strong, capable of turning the other cheek even when struck by a fist. By contrast, the man in the kitchen had ministered his flock with visions of brimstone and the condemnation of hellfire. His sermons had been delivered in a stentorian clamor from a creaky wooden pulpit in the dilapidated Pentecostal church at the edge of town.

The memories still brought a chill to her heart. She often wakened with his voice ringing in her ears. She could almost imagine his charismatic baritone resonating with the spiritual desire to bring converts over the chasm of righteousness through baptism-by-water. Her stepfather hadn't acted so righteous at the end.

"Talk to me, Lainie."

The Sheriff's voice sounded far away but the words emptied out of her mouth in response. "I was six, already half an orphan when Mama brought him into the house." She peered around the room, recognized the familiar stone fireplace on the north wall and the lace curtains on the small windows flanking the front entry, and felt whole. "I've been too long away."

Bitterwater lived up to its name. Established at the close of the nineteenth century, back when desperate land grubbers still believed it was possible to grow corn in the wind-scoured landscape, the town teetered for decades on the verge of expiring. The pendulum swung with each generation. Kids graduated from high school and fled to the city, only to return one-at-a-time in a reverse migration when the ache for a simpler life grew in their hearts. Worn looks stamped their faces and hunger churned in their bellies but Bitterwater welcomed each one home.

Lainie's voice cracked for the first time, "He buried mama in the garden patch next to the shed. She's lying beneath the Buffalo Berry bushes he made me plant right before he sent me to the state home."

Sheriff Dunsteady swore softly.

She didn't mind. She'd long ago accepted some emotional releases required cursing.

"How'd you get back?"

A glance at the clock showed almost six minutes had passed. Like a wild bird following an ancestral memory, she'd flown east from Alliance, seeking the place of her birth. "I hitched a ride from a nice truck driver. He worried about dropping me alone on the outskirts of town."

The Sheriff made a rumble of sound that might have been agreement or disapproval. "I remember your mama, Lainie. She was a good-hearted woman."

The words softened the images in her memory. In her mind mama always wept, worn down by her demanding husband, her beauty claimed by sorrow over his distrustful accusations. "I never believed she went into the frosty night without taking any of her personal things, or writing a note, and especially leaving me behind. Her car sat cold in the driveway, Sheriff. Didn't anybody wonder about that?"

The armature on the turntable reset. The song started to play a third time.

"I know it's no excuse but he was a man of the cloth. We believed him."

Sheriff Dunsteady's words rang in her ear, the receiver weighed heavy in her hand.

"In Bitterwater we pride ourselves on taking care of our own. We failed you once, Lainie, we won't do it again."

The patrol car pulled up outside.

She began to sing the words of the song.

When the Sheriff's gravelly voice joined hers, she knew she was finally home.

10   ESCAPING JUSTICE

WEDNESDAY AFTERNOON INCHED to a close. Sheriff Bill Johns checked the clock for the third time in half an hour. He was ready to wind down. Almost done. Soon he could cross off another square on the calendar. He was one more day closer to retirement.

The office quieted as staff departed at the end of the dayshift. Budget cuts left only a skeleton crew working nights. Good thing the crime rate had dropped along with the population. A new era of law enforcement had arrived and the managerial style was not to his taste. The county too would soon get a contemporary figurehead and he could give a shit about that as well.

The latest green-behind-the-ears Public Relations Officer spoke near his shoulder.

"I guess you never forget the one that got away."

The Sheriff ignored the PRO until the man gave up attempting small talk and carried his clipboard out to the main office. The sounds of a file cabinet drawer opening and closing drifted through the open door. The swish of coffee as someone emptied the carafe, another indication of closure, seemed oddly out of place. The audio track was familiar, as much a part of his daily routine as any other aspect of his personal or professional life, but he could scarce stand to hear them now.

Instead he focused on the framed newspaper clipping.

This was his last week on the job. The office walls were nearly bared of the accumulated debris of four decades on the clock. The printed article was the only personal object remaining.

He'd deliberately left this chore for last.

The words spelled out across the top of the page shone stark under the fluorescent lights. He didn't really need to read them. After so many years he could recite not only the headline, but the entire first paragraph.

The PRO tapped past, his polished loafers clicking against the scuffed industrial tiles on the floor. The Sheriff stepped forward and closed the door, exerting the perfect amount of pressure to make the steel-framed panel swing shut and latch. He felt too old to understand the new generation of cops the County Supervisory Commission kept hiring. Their method of doing business just pissed him off. Everything stipulated by-the-book. No more gray areas. No second chances. No extenuating circumstances. Nothing to make a man second-guess the guilty from the innocent.

Once he'd been like that too but experience had taught him the cost of lacking compassion.

The bold block letters were easily read from his desk chair but he walked over to stand in front of the framed article. For twenty years he'd stared at the words and let them seep deeply into his guilty conscience. He allowed them to become a constant reminder of the one selfless act he'd performed because doing so let him reach a step closer to absolution.

His long career, punctuated by many successes, featured one spectacular failure. He had not captured the only multiple murderer the county had ever produced. The miss had been a stain on his reputation, a dark one.

He considered the miscarriage of justice his personal penance.

The town turned that boy into a killer. When Paul Branson finally snapped and retaliated against the bullies, the sadists, and the pejorative two-faced preaching of the righteous, his violent rage shouldn't have surprised anyone. The townsfolk pulled on stunned faces but the expressions were as unconvincing as the pundits on the evening news.

The Sheriff had experienced a life-altering epiphany at the very first crime scene.

"You reap what you sow."

His muttered words were loud in his empty office but he was lost in memory.

The public had sown hate in the form of young Paul. The boy had been punished for being born of an unwed mother and a wastrel father, as if he'd any choice in the matter. By the age of fourteen his dad had run off and his mom barely scrimped together the money to feed her habits every month, much less take proper care of her son. People took the poor kid to task for wearing ragged clothes and second-hand cast-offs instead of offering assistance.

No one intervened.

The boy had been watered with pity and fertilized with scorn.

They were *all* at fault and the Sheriff topped the list with his own name. After all, it was his job to intercede.

He hadn't.

When the carnage ended, Paul Branson disappeared into the woods.

The Sheriff found his trail and tracked him deep into the high country but his heart hadn't been in the pursuit. In the end, he'd let the boy go. To his way of thinking, the scales of justice weighed off-balance every time he considered taking the fugitive into custody, especially when the town itself would never be held accountable for such criminal neglect.

The rain smoothed away any traces of passage.

The Sheriff claimed there were no tracks to be found and wrote the lack of details into the official record.

The town buried the victims in somber quiet graveside ceremonies. Residents learned to lock their doors. A tragic lesson, the pastor spoke in a sermon a month later, prevailing on the congregation to pray for salvation and the fugitive's capture.

That was the last day the Sheriff ever attended church.

The domino effect continued through the years. Families touched by the tragedy packed up and left town. Businesses closed as the economy tightened. Each graduation from the high school signaled the departure of the next generation. Eventually there weren't enough children to maintain the schools and the district also shuttered its doors. The health clinic outlasted the others by four months.

The town died.

Nobody else seemed to understand why.

Two more days of driving the twenty-six miles to his desk at the county office before his offer of official employment expired. Forty-eight hours until he signed out his gun for the last time and locked it up in the drawer of the bedside table. Less than 3,000 minutes before he struck his badge number from the duty roster and headed up the mountain to his retirement.

Next week Bill Johns planned a celebration for this twilight of his life. A hike out the narrow ridge he'd followed all those years ago. He'd look for wildlife and other signs of passage. Fortune might favor his efforts and show him the location of a trail, maybe one that would lead to the plume of smoke he spied through his field glasses every winter. If he was lucky enough to find Paul Branson, he'd tell the man all about his regrets. He'd offer his apologies and indicate how much he wanted to sit down and listen to his side of things.

11 THE MAN IN THE DARK SUIT

BETHANY LITKOWSKI TRAWLED the room with the eyes of a professional courtesan. With a pat on the shoulder and the touch of her fingers, she baited hooks for Brian to reel in new clients. It was the typical crowd for one of the parties the law firm annually hosted, the kind of gathering filled with wealthy insincere potential.

She wedged herself between her next mark and his date.

The nubile girl swaying beside Quentin Baxter was barely post-pubescent but the dramatic white gown draped strategically over her high round breasts gaped open to her navel in a fabulous display of skin. She wore the slinky fabric like it was taped to her nipples. For two seconds the visual made

Bethany feel the weight of every one of her twenty-nine years, then she dismissed the child and focused on her target.

Her insinuation that Quentin's legal interests would be better served by Brian's careful attention to detail scored his interest. He sent the cheerleader scampering toward the champagne fountain for refills. Several men turned to follow her progress but Quentin only had eyes for the elegant woman at his side.

Hooked.

Adept at reading sensitive shifts in emotion, Bethany heard the innuendo in his tone of voice and capitalized on his attraction by extracting a time and date to schedule a formal phone consultation. At this rate her husband would not be a minor partner for long. She'd made a practice of poaching clients on his behalf and the lack of a prenuptial agreement meant she benefited by default.

Bethany was an accomplished liar, one of the best in a room filled with six-figure lawyers. That was the single personality facet she'd failed to hide from her obtuse husband during thirty-six months of marriage. On more than one occasion he'd praised her skill in deception as a worthy asset to Team Litkowski.

The barely-of-legal-age escort, witnessing Quentin's speculative eye roving over Bethany's tall pale beauty, stalked a return path across the room. Her black leather heels spiked tiny depressions in the carpet. She moved like a runway model, expensive bubbly slopping over the rims of the glasses to glisten on her red-tipped fingernails.

Bethany turned away before the girl arrived, a smile of success curving her plump lips.

A familiar hand stroked across her shoulder. Brian let his fingers trail down to her elbow. "It's your turn."

She hated these word games more than the fact she topped him by half a head in height. "You go first."

He smiled and pulled her close, tucked her into his side, one pudgy arm snaking around her waist as he addressed the room. "I would put my lovely wife's picture in the dictionary next to *scintillation*."

There was a round of applause. Several women simpered at the silly entertainment and shot meaningful glares at their spouses.

Bethany swallowed a grimace and thought a more appropriate word would be fraud. She froze the amused smile on her mouth and looked down at her spouse. Brian Litzkowski's bland face was wreathed in happy anticipation. For a fast second she wanted to claim she'd put his picture next to simpleton, instead she played nice. "Brian is *generous*."

The insipid effort brought the expected vocal approval and a twinge of guilt pulled her down to kiss his cheek. It was true, in a way. Brian had provided every last thing she needed: a new identity, a safe place to hide, and an existence so boring it was hardly worth getting dressed in the morning.

He squeezed her arm and stepped away. "I'll get you some wine."

She watched him cross the room, short legs moving like pistons, his blocky shape filling out the dark suit with surprising elegance. Sometimes she didn't know what to make of the man she'd married. Brian would return with a plate of party nibbles and a glass of white zinfandel. Beside her ability to work a crowd, the food and drink preferences were the only parts of the real Bethany Litzkowski he knew.

She smiled and nodded at the guests, chatted and made small talk like always but inside she screamed. She worried that one day soon she'd be unable to choke back the lies. They might simply escape in an ongoing ululation of sound from deep in her being.

That was the moment her past burst through the elevator door. He wore denim pants and a white button-down shirt with a European collar. Sunglasses propped atop his curly black hair, the lenses catching and reflecting light from the fluorescent bulbs overhead.

Bethany turned to stone at the sight of the armed man. Her breath escaped in a rush of recognition.

His angry shouted words echoed a heavy Sicilian accent and any doubt about his intent evaporated when he screamed her name. Faces in the crowd darted frightened glances toward her and shuffled away.

Soon she stood alone.

Behind her the wall of humanity arced out to frame her like a sacrificial goat offered by a peasant in supplication to an angry deity.

Bethany swore under her breath. This was one of Pietro's grandsons, hell bent on avenging the old guy's honor. It wasn't fair to hold her responsible for the patriarch's poor financial decisions, even if she had suggested he invest in that offshore enterprise. She'd come out well but he'd taken the losses hard. The network built by generations of Cosa Nostra had traced her across an ocean and the crowded Los Angeles basin. That was no mean feat.

A curse in guttural Italian split the silence. The words flipped over the hourglass for the final countdown on Bethany's existence.

The gun swept the room, the assailant's arm held straight out like an accusing finger until it pointed at her chest.

Death would be swift at least. She supposed the end of life offered a resolution of sorts. The upside meant no more strain or deception. Bethany squeezed her eyelids shut and found comfort in knowing that Brian would mourn her passing. Her dumpy husband had wormed his way into her slate heart. That was something.

The blast hurt her ears. The dual report of two rapidly fired shots deafened her hearing. Her vision swam. The thunder of her heartbeat drowned out all sound and the room spun as she fought the faint. Then she blinked and focused. The body of the Italian was sprawled in a grotesque tangle of limbs on the floor. A red stain ripened over his chest and confusion replaced her fear.

Brian circled her limp form with one arm and clasping her tightly to his ribs, lowered her gently to the carpet.

Bethany clutched at him, her hands tightening on his black suit coat. She tried to slide her eyes away from the dull glint of the handgun but the .45 looked huge in his small hand. She couldn't correlate the visuals or make sense of what had just occurred. The smell of cordite burned her nostrils. Her mouth went slack. A squeak of sound erupted from her chest.

A stampede of people sought escape. They poured into the elevator and down the stairwell, desperate to depart the scene and the legal aftermath.

Bethany's gaze finally locked on her husband's eyes. She stammered out the obvious. "You. Shot. Him."

Brian swept a gentle hand over the crown of her head, smoothing down a wisp of honey gold hair. He grinned. It was the same smile he wore on the occasions he departed for court, especially during high-profile trials.

"When the police arrive, let me do the talking, Bethany. I'm a defense attorney. Most of my clients are educated men in positions of authority with enviable social status." He scanned a heated look down her body. "I know a quality criminal when I see one."

Bethany flushed. "I'm sorry. I lied about everything."

He lifted her hand and kissed her fingertips. "Really darling, how else could a short bald guy land such a gorgeous trophy wife?"

12 THE CARPENTER'S CASE

DETECTIVE PAOLO CABRERA issued explicit instructions to the ward nurse at the station desk. The woman studied him with polite detachment until he voiced the name of the patient and then her eyes flickered with emotion. He hoped she'd obey his directive when the time came. In response to his query, she pointed to the east wing. The air was cold and stale. The underlayment of harsh chemical cleaners teased his nostrils. A miasma of despair was palpable.

The muscular orderlies prowling the corridors ignored him. The menace projected in his demeanor intimidated the residents and sent them scurrying out of his path. He approached the wing with the private hospital rooms. Each step carried him closer to discharging his duty.

Tension vibrated up his spine.

Countless cycles of night and day had passed in an unfathomable procession of sameness since Robert Stinson had been committed under the influence of his wealthy and powerful surname. Almost thirty-nine years had been logged on the institutional records for patient #3612. Cabrera suspected nearly four decades of an existence filtered through the lens of anti-psychotic drugs would prepare even a sane person to embrace the grave.

Mortality had run its course.

He was here to bear witness. The motivation that spurred him to confront the man who'd changed hundreds of lives, altered dozens of personal histories, and reshaped entire families stemmed from more than professional angst. The unit was the last one at the far end of the hall.

Perfect.

Cabrera paused outside the opaque safety-glass of the door marked NC4. He wanted this moment to feel momentous. The cold case investigation he'd re-opened after making detective had led to an empty windowless chamber in a Fifth Avenue mansion owned by the Stinson family. The vast structure had been constructed in the Beaux-Arts style popularized at the turn of the century in the United States. The monstrous architectural building was the kind of American castle favored by documentary film-makers as an example of the golden age of entrepreneurial spirit. Sculptural decorations reminiscent of Baroque and Rococo elements were integrated in the over-scaled details. The grand motifs, balustrades and pilasters had harbored a monster amid the splendor.

Cabrera adjusted the weight hanging from his fingers. The wooden box had sat centered under a chandelier crafted by the renowned Louis Tiffany. The intricately pieced stained glass mosaic had rivaled the ones framing the governor's mansion that featured prominently in publicity stills during election years. Fractured multicolored beams of sunlight illuminated the heavy oak grain of the carpenter's case and contrasted the molasses tones of the polished mahogany table on which it rested. The hinged top opened to display the eerie contents and the choreographed celebration of death still sickened Cabrera.

Interior items were neatly arranged by category. Slips of paper labeled in a precise exquisitely formed script annotated a name. He'd spent hours poring over each one and correlating them with the list of known victims. In the end, solid police work and the killer's own distinctive violent tendencies had not missed a connection. The hand that shaped every letter had been educated in the finest schools, presented the best opportunities, and encouraged along avenues guaranteed to achieve success; instead, the Upper East Side heir had chosen the cobbled road to hell.

Focus returned to the present, Cabrera pushed through the door.

The wasted form of a man lay on a narrow mechanical bed. Machines seemed to fill the remaining available space. Stout restraints manacled his wrists and ankles, limiting all movement. Age had bleached Stinson's hair to match the pale color of his flesh. He turned his head and displayed dark eyes deeply-set in a cadaverous face. His pupils were dull and unfocused.

Cabrera guessed inactivity had sucked the muscle from the man's body, atrophied limbs appeared arachnoid in nature, almost disproportionate to the scale of his torso.

The invalid's gaze locked on the object in Cabrera's grasp. The sight of the case transformed his expression. A feverish bevy of alarms sounded from the equipment beside the bed. Red and yellow warnings flashed. The needle on the respiration graph danced back and forth. The heart monitor twitched steadily upward in a lethal ascent. The blip following the patient's fibrillating chambers ramped across the screen. The radiograph line staggered into peaks and valleys. Codes echoed insistently in the cold space.

Fierce satisfaction licked through Cabrera. He hefted his burden atop a wheeled instrument cart.

Stinson's eyes followed the movement, glittering in the glow of flickering lights. A rictus of pleased anticipation curled his lips. "Let me see." He said.

The hoarse command carried an element of power and the voice, a lingering vestige of the charisma that had charmed countless victims. Tremulous fingers reached and failed, checked by the heavy nylon wrist band.

Concealing his revulsion, Cabrera splayed a palm toward the oak box in the manner of a practiced showman but he couldn't bring himself to smile. "You amassed an interesting collection."

His tone was too soft to carry beyond the sterile space. The simple sentence contained a trace of his mother's Dominican cadence, a lament for the dead, recognition that all would be different but for the chance finger of fate.

Stinson's focus never left the burnished container. "Open the lid."

With slow movements Cabrera unlatched the two halves of the top and lowered the front panel. Inside were numerous objects. Piles of simple childish toys collectively offered a glimpse into the anarchy within Robert Stinson's damaged psyche.

Stinson stared for long moments.

When he spoke, the words resonated in the room. "My work was unfinished. Others seldom aspire to true creative vision." A brittle laugh spilled out his mouth. A second later Stinson flicked out his tongue and tasted the air, a snake testing for an elusive flavor.

Cabrera wondered how many generations back the madness had first bloomed. Surely this degree of depravity could not flower from a single source?

"The block-cut figures commemorate the soldiers I released to the river." Stinson pointed with a flick of his fingers.

The police archives listed the names of eleven servicemen dragged out of the East River. Every individual had been all but decapitated in gratuitous displays of violence. The coroner reports had given rise to the title due to the dexterity of how the culprit wielded a blade. Like other notorious felons before him, the suspected murderer was thought to perhaps have received surgical training. The newspapers had dubbed him The Carpenter. The public records mounted as victim after victim was claimed.

Cabrera scrutinized the medical equipment. Lights blinked. Alarms sounded. Monitors redlined. His directive to ignore distress signals was being honored. He prompted the old man. "Tell me about the porcelain doll heads." The jumble of white faces was disquieting to view in the green velvet lining of the interior.

Stinson uttered a sound of pleasure. "Ah, yes. The mementos of my ladies." His tongue caressed the phonemes in each word as he pronounced the syllables with eloquent attention. "I selected them with such care, sought to capture an individual likeness. Their lovely blue orbs demanded fitting tribute." Stinson focused on the petite smooth white craniums inside the wooden case. Lust twisted his features.

Cabrera swallowed the rush of fluid in his mouth.

The files on the women encompassed an entire block of shelves in the records department. He'd spent months reading the details of the crimes, after-hours and on his days off. Stinson had favored blondes. Horrific photographs documented the nineteen mutilated females in gruesome clarity. The stark greyscale snapshots showed the empty bleeding eye sockets in graphic detail, the feature that was Stinson's signature.

"I want to know about Sarah Lambert." Cabrera said.

Stinson heard the emotion in his intonation. Like a hound scenting blood his gaze swiveled to Cabrera. An expectant grin displayed perfect teeth. "My gilded swan. My final masterpiece."

The drawled words clutched at Cabrera's chest, prying between his ribs like spectral fingers to squeeze his lungs and steal his breath.

"The crystal beads on the bodice of her wedding gown glittered in the morning sunlight. I was careful to keep the blood off her dress. Did you know the family buried her in that frock? I always liked that detail. I remember thinking that she lay so graceful on the steps of St. Michel's Church, serene as a swan. The scene would have made a lovely painting. I broke her neck and took her eyes instead." Pleasure rippled across Stinson's face.

Cabrera decided the time had come to conclude this business. He reached down, gathered up a handful of power cords and yanked. The bank of noisy machinery fell silent.

"The official admission records chronicle your involuntary commitment in this facility on the same day Sarah died."

Stinson rolled his eyes since he couldn't shrug his shoulders from a prone position. His gaze never strayed long from his trophies.

"My parents disapproved my vocation. The Lambert family being friends and all, made it awkward for them, I suppose." He wheezed contemptuous laughter, his lips turning blue as he labored to inhale each successive breath into his wasted body. "What does anyone care after so many years?"

Cabrera approached the bed and stood staring down at the most prolific serial killer the city had ever spawned.

"There is no statute of limitations on murder, but that is not why I am here." He swept one arm toward the carpenter's case, simultaneously sending up a prayer for forgiveness. "This is a gift I give to you."

Confusion etched Stinson's waxen features.

The detective leaned closer until he filled Stinson's field of vision. "Sarah Lambert was my father's fiancée. You changed the course of his history too. I exist only because you killed her." He held the dying man's gaze. "Today we complete the cycle of sacrifice and retribution."

Comprehension flooded Stinson's features.

Cabrera savored the flicker of fear he saw in the aged killer's face as Stinson's heart seized.

ABOUT LESANN BERRY

As an anthropologist, Lesann divides her time between academic interests and professional research. Focused primarily on the American west, she is inspired by the geologic features of empty landscapes. The ancient art and prehistory of those settings often feature in her work. She writes about messed-up people and sinister events, saying her stories often feature paranormal or romantic elements because life is boring without spooky stuff and warm bodies. Crossing genre lines, she pens both contemporary and historical mysteries, romantic suspense, and even a little horror.

Visit WWW.LESANNBERRY.COM for new releases.

www.ingramcontent.com/pod-product-compliance
Lightning Source LLC
Chambersburg PA
CBHW020630130626
46552CB00003B/1152